VENGEANCE

THE TRANSCEND TIME SAGA: PART TWO

MICHELLE MADOW

Want the first book in Michelle Madow's Elementals series FOR FREE?

Go to www.michellemadow.com/free-elementals and claim your free book!

"I'll see you in school on Monday."

I hated the casual way Lizzie said those words. She was acting like she hadn't stolen my boyfriend, come over to apologize, and expected us to be best friends as if nothing had changed. It made me want to throw the stapler on my desk at her face. Instead, I glanced at my planner and shuffled a few papers around as if they needed to be rearranged. They didn't.

"Right," I said, refusing to look at her. I wanted Lizzie to leave. Every second I saw her made me angrier than the last.

She watched me like she expected me to say more—like she expected me to tell her I couldn't wait to see her at school. When I didn't, she turned around and left. I could tell she was disappointed, but what did she expect? She knew I was interested in Drew from the first time I saw him walk into our History classroom. I'd been honest with her about my feelings for him from the beginning.

When Drew and I started dating, everything was great, like a fairy tale. Whenever we spent time together, whether we went out for ice cream, dinner, or watched a movie at my house, we had fun. At least I thought we did.

But apparently he enjoyed Lizzie's company more than mine.

I pushed the red mask I wore to the Halloween Dance off the desk and watched it fall to the floor. Then I kicked it into the wall for added effect. Stupid mask. The night of the dance was supposed to be incredible. Then Drew cancelled so he could see his family in New York for the weekend, and when he came back he was distant. His mind was somewhere else—somewhere I couldn't reach. No matter how hard I tried to get him to lighten up, it was impossible.

He broke up with me two weeks later. I saw it coming, but that didn't make it less devastating. I didn't understand what I'd done to make him so uninterested in me. When I asked, he gave me the "it's not you, it's me" excuse, as if that would make it okay. It was so lame, so cliché—he could have given me a decent reason. A *real* reason. One minute he was happy with our relationship, and the next he was done with me, tossing me aside like I never mattered to him in the first place.

Shannon pulled me aside a week later and told me she saw Drew and Lizzie together in a boat on the lake behind their houses. I didn't want to believe her at first. But both of them were acting strange and secretive—it was the only explanation that made sense. I couldn't help but wonder how long they planned on keeping their relationship from everyone.

Then there was the biggest, most hurtful question of them all: How long had they been seeing each other behind my back before Drew broke up with me?

I hated thinking about it.

I tried talking with him about it at Shannon's party, but as soon as I started getting somewhere, Lizzie barged in and ruined everything. Drew ran after her, leaving me alone and forgotten. It was humiliating.

I walked up to the mirror in my room and glared at my reflection. What was so wrong with me that I wasn't good enough for Drew? That he left me for my best friend—correction: my ex-best friend—without looking back?

I ran a hand through my long, dark hair, trying to figure it out. My nose had a perfect ski-slope shape that people went to plastic surgeons for, my skin was smooth and free of any blemishes, and my green eyes tilted upwards at the ends in a way that guys found alluring. I didn't doubt that I was prettier than Lizzie. Her curly hair was constantly out of control, her skin was too pale, and she looked like she should be a freshman instead of a junior.

Despite all of that, Drew chose her. And Lizzie went along with it. She knew about my feelings for Drew—how I *loved* Drew—and she still took him away from me. Then she had the nerve to come into my house and tell me she thought Drew was her soul mate and she hoped I understood where she was coming from.

The last thing I wanted was to be friends with her. To top things off, it wasn't the first time something like this had happened. At least it was forgivable all those years ago with Jeremy, since I never told Lizzie about my feelings for him in the first place. Jeremy was different from other guys—he was one of my close friends. I was afraid if I let him know I thought there could be more between us, it would mess up our friendship. So I kept it to myself.

In eighth grade he told me he wanted to ask Lizzie to the Valentine's Day dance. Not knowing how to respond, I froze and told him I thought it would be a great idea. They went to the dance together, and in less than a month they were an official couple. He never knew about my feelings for him, and I always thought it was best that way. He and Lizzie were good together. It was my fault for not taking action sooner, and I wasn't about to get between them. I got over him a few months later.

But with Drew ... this was a different situation. Lizzie knew about my feelings for him, but she went for him anyway. Everyone might think Lizzie's an angel, but I knew better. She was selfish, and she was going to pay.

Still staring in the mirror, I made myself a promise.

I was going to get revenge.

CHAPTER 2

*M*y cell phone buzzed on my nightstand, waking me up the next morning. I turned over to check the clock, groaning when I saw it was 11:00 AM. I couldn't fall asleep last night because I kept thinking about everything that had happened with Drew and Lizzie at the party on Friday, and how my chances of getting him back looked like they were slim to none. I just wanted to lie in bed all day, watch sad romance movies, and maybe get some homework done. Anything to keep my mind off Drew and Lizzie.

I glanced at the caller ID and saw it was Shannon. She wasn't the type of person who liked to be ignored, so I picked up the phone and answered it.

"What's up?" I asked, my voice hoarse from just waking up.

"Hey, Chelsea. We're going to the mall today," she

said. If she noticed how she woke me up, she didn't let on.

"When?" I rubbed my eyes and flopped over in bed. My white pillowcase was covered with black smudge marks since I'd forgotten to take off my makeup the night before. Hopefully it wouldn't stain.

"Whenever you're ready," she said, her voice chirpy and bright.

"You never struck me as a morning person," I grumbled.

She ignored my comment. "So, I'll pick you up in thirty minutes?"

Apparently I was going to the mall today, whether I liked it or not.

I had to give Shannon some credit though—I was happy someone was reaching out to me. She was the one who stayed with me at her party when I cried in the bathroom for an hour after Drew chased after Lizzie. I didn't understand the motives behind her sudden kindness, but I appreciated it. Lizzie was usually the one who helped me through tough times, but since she couldn't help when she was the one making me upset, I was glad Shannon could. Plus, I loved the mall. Maybe a trip there *would* help me feel better about this mess.

"That sounds good." I tried to put some gratitude into my tone. "I'll see you soon."

I managed to get out of bed and changed into jeans and a red, long-sleeved shirt. Red was my best color, and even though it was only a mall trip with Shannon, I still wanted to look good. I put on some light makeup—nothing too extreme since it was daytime—and was ready to go with ten minutes to spare.

I went downstairs to say hi to my dad, but he was nowhere to be found. That was strange, since he was normally up by now, drinking a cup of coffee and reading the Sunday paper. I did find a note that he left, letting me know he had gone out for breakfast and would be back soon.

I wondered who he had gone out with. My dad had been doing this a lot recently—going out to get food and being vague about his company. I couldn't help thinking there was a possibility he was dating. He hadn't been on many dates since my mom passed away when I was in third grade. No one would ever be able to replace her, but I would be happy if he was making an effort to get himself out there. I'd been telling him he should for years.

I didn't have much time to think about it before my cell phone buzzed in my back pocket.

I'm outside, the text from Shannon read.

On my way out, I replied. I grabbed my jacket and gloves from the front closet and put them on before leaving the house, watching out for patches of ice on the sidewalk as I headed towards Shannon's Lexus SUV. She had on huge pink designer sunglasses, and her short blonde hair was ironed straight, not a strand out of place.

"You're looking better," she said as I got into the car, lowering the pop music blaring from her speakers.

"Thanks," I said, even though I felt anything but. These past few weeks, full of rejection from the two people I cared most about in the world, had worn me out more than I ever thought possible.

I didn't say anything for a few seconds. Then Shannon asked, "So, have you talked to Drew since the party?"

"No." I shook my head and gazed out the window, not wanting to think about Friday night more than I had to. "I almost called him a few times, but it felt too pathetic. I'm not going to be that girl who won't stop calling her ex and annoys him to death."

"Good move," she agreed. "You don't want to make him happy about breaking up with you."

"Definitely not," I said. "But I do want him to regret it."

Shannon raised an eyebrow. "Did you have anything in mind?" she asked.

"I was up for a while last night trying to think of

something," I started, glad she was willing to listen. She even seemed on board to help. I wasn't sure why she cared, but I did like having someone to talk with about it all.

"And ..." she prodded.

"Nothing." I sighed and sat back in the seat. "All my ideas seemed lame—finding someone else to date to make him jealous, telling him I'm okay being friends with him and then having him regret breaking up with me in the first place, or wearing hot outfits to school to make sure he notices me. I couldn't think of anything that would work. And I have this feeling, even though it doesn't make sense, that this wasn't supposed to be how things ended with us. That we're supposed to be together. It sounds nuts, and I feel like an idiot for thinking it, but I can't shake the idea that everything happening now is wrong. It's all off, and I can't explain why."

Shannon pressed her glossed lips together and nodded, like she wasn't sure how to respond.

"I know it sounds crazy," I said. "Forget it."

"No." Shannon shook her head and tapped her French manicured fingernails on the steering wheel. "That's all very interesting. In fact, I might be able to help."

That wasn't what I was expecting. "If you have any

ideas, I'm willing to listen," I said. "I need all the help I can get."

"Alright." She flipped her short blonde hair over her shoulder and looked at me before turning her attention back to the road. "This might sound strange, but hear me out. Have you ever seen that store in the mall, Mystic Pathways?"

"The one with the crystals in the display windows?" I asked. I'd seen the store and even been inside it once—but that was a few years ago, with Lizzie as a joke. I still remembered it clearly though. It was dark inside, and full of beads, old books, and unidentifiable herbs. Plus, the lady who worked there was strange. She reminded me of the old scary women in fairytales—the ones who give candy to children before kidnapping them and cooking them in the oven.

"That's the one." Shannon nodded. "My great-aunt owns it. She's into all that magic stuff. Promise you won't tell anyone though, cause it's not something I publicize around school."

"Hold up a minute." I tried not to laugh at the thought that popped into my mind. "Are you saying your aunt thinks she's a *witch*?"

"No!" Shannon exclaimed. "Don't be ridiculous. She's not a witch. She's more like … well, I guess if you want an exact term, you could call her a psychic. And she can help you."

I stared at her in shock, but she stayed focused on the road. Not that I could blame her. What she said was embarrassing. I mean, come on. She wanted me to believe her aunt is a *psychic*? Last night I told Lizzie that fairy tales and soul mates and supernatural stuff doesn't exist, and I meant every word of it. Now I'm supposed to believe Shannon's aunt is a psychic who owns a mystical shop in the mall, and that she can help me put Lizzie in her place?

"That sounds crazy," I said.

"I know," Shannon agreed. "But didn't you say that you and Drew were supposed to be together, and Lizzie messed everything up?"

"I did," I admitted. "But it was stupid. It would be nice if fate was real, but it isn't."

Shannon pulled the car into the mall parking lot and started to search for a space. "Are you one hundred percent sure?" she asked.

I just don't believe in it." I shrugged. "I've never seen anything to prove it could exist. It would be nice if it did, but I can't force myself to believe in something that I don't think is true."

"I wouldn't believe it either, but in the beginning of the school year my aunt cornered me at a family dinner,"

Shannon said. A car nearby started to back out, and she put on her turn signal to reserve the spot. "She told me a boy was going to transfer into our school, and he was going to start dating a girl, but there was a chance he would leave this girl for someone else. She said when that happened, she wanted me to bring the first girl to her. Doesn't that sound like what happened with you, Drew, and Lizzie?"

"It does." I chewed on my pink-painted thumbnail as Shannon parked. "But it's so vague. Stuff like that happens all the time in school. It's more likely this was coincidence—not that your aunt is a psychic who predicted everything that was going to happen between the three of us. It makes no sense."

"I know it doesn't," she said, yanking her keys out of the ignition and turning toward me. "But I promise my aunt is better at explaining it than I am. Can you at least give her a chance? If after you talk to her you still don't believe it, I'll drop it. But you never know—maybe she can help. And none of your other ideas were any good. You can use all the help you can get." She narrowed her eyes in her trademark intimidating way, and I knew I didn't have much of a choice—at least if I wanted to stay friends with her.

"Fine." I huffed. "I'll give it a chance. But don't get your hopes up. Magical stuff isn't my thing."

"And telling people that I'm related to someone who's into 'magical stuff' isn't my thing either, but my aunt told me to tell you, so I'm listening to her," Shannon said. "Just don't tell anyone at school. If you do … well, let's just say you'll regret it." She raised a plucked eyebrow and smirked to let me know she was joking. But even though I'd only been friends with Shannon for a few weeks, I knew not to piss her off. If there was a "Queen Bee" at school, she was it. Making her angry would be social suicide. I'd hit a new low when my boyfriend dumped me for my best friend, and I wasn't about to make my life worse by making the most popular girl at school hate me.

"I won't tell anyone," I promised. "I don't want anyone to know I was in that store, either."

"I'm glad we have an agreement." Shannon tossed her hair over her shoulder and opened the door to get out of the car. "Remember to keep an open mind. It's not very often my aunt wants to help someone so much, so at least try to take her seriously."

I followed her into the mall, wondering what on Earth I was getting myself into.

CHAPTER 3

*M*ystic Pathways hadn't changed since the time I went in there a few years ago with Lizzie. The thin carpet was forest green, the walls were dark wood, and the lighting was so dim that it took a few seconds for my eyes to adjust. There were no ceiling lights, only lamps on top of the multi-level wooden tables that held strange knick-knacks. The shelves on the walls were stocked with old books, and there were spices and herbs near the back. Two college-aged girls dressed in earth-toned clothing perused crystals on a nearby table, but other than that, the store was empty.

"Is your aunt even here today?" I asked, keeping my voice low so I wouldn't grab the attention of the girls. The last thing I needed was for them to walk up to us and try to start a conversation about potions and herbs, or whatever they talked about for fun.

"She's probably in the back," Shannon said. She headed toward the old wooden desk at the back of the room and pressed the bell next to the cash register—the kind they have at hotels when you want to get the attention of the concierge.

The door in the back creaked open, and an old lady hobbled out. She moved slowly toward us, balancing on the cane she held in her shaking hand. Her wrinkly skin was so pale it was almost translucent, and even though it was dark in the store, I could see the blue veins popping out on the top of her hands. She wore one of those shapeless dresses fat women wear, even though she was so thin that a breeze could knock her over. Her wispy gray hair was cut above her shoulders, and when she looked at me I shuddered at the sight of her milky eyes. It didn't seem possible she could see, but she managed to continue forward, the cane clomping against the floor with each step she took.

When she reached us she studied me, then turned her attention to Shannon.

"I see you've brought a friend," she said, her papery lips quivering as she spoke. "Would you care to introduce us?"

"This is Chelsea." Shannon motioned toward me.

"We're in school together. Chelsea, this is my great-aunt Genevieve. She's the one I was telling you about—the one who owns the store."

The way Genevieve looked at us both at once was creepy, like she could focus on different things with each eye. Goosebumps prickled over my arms, even though it wasn't cold.

"Any particular reason why you brought Chelsea to me?" Genevieve asked Shannon. She did a motion that I guessed would be raising an eyebrow, if she had any hair where her eyebrows should be.

"Yes." Shannon cleared her throat and continued, "Remember a few months ago when you told me you wanted me to bring someone in to meet you? I think Chelsea's the one you were referring to."

"Really?" Genevieve turned her attention to me, and her cloudy eyes took on a sharper quality, as if she was seeing me for the first time. She stepped forward and grabbed my hand, her skin cold and coarse. I flinched, surprised by her touch, but her grip was stronger than I expected. Then she pressed her fingers into my palm and closed her eyes, deep in concentration.

I was starting to wonder why I'd agreed to come here in the first place. It wasn't like this old lady could do anything to improve my situation. Still, I would bear through it, because Shannon wanted me to.

"I sense that you're angry," Genevieve finally said. Her voice was calmer than before, as if she was under a trance. "You've been betrayed by those you trusted the most."

"Yeah." I shifted from one foot to the other. I didn't know if she wanted me to believe she was psychic from one observation, but I wasn't that gullible. I tried to tug my hand out of her grip, but she held on firmly, not allowing me to let go.

"Not so fast," she said. "This isn't the first time you've lived out these experiences. There was another time, nearly two centuries ago, when something similar happened to you. However, there was quite a different ending to your story then. Now you have been reborn, and things aren't working out the way you hoped."

Reborn? That was impossible. I tried again to pull my hand out of hers, successfully this time.

"Seriously?" I said. "That stuff is cool in stories and all, but just ... no. No way. That's not possible."

"You said you would keep an open mind," Shannon insisted.

"That was before I was told I had a past life." I threw my hands in the air, amazed by the ridiculousness of all this.

"You're the one who said you couldn't shake the feeling that everything happening to you was wrong, and it wasn't supposed to end up this way," she pointed out. "What if you do have a past life? My aunt can help you remember."

"No." I shook my head. "It's too out there to even think about it."

"Come on, dear," Genevieve said. "Shannon's right. Listen to what I have to say. There are ways I can help you. You can regain control of what's going on in your life, and change things back to the way they were supposed to be." I remained silent, which I suppose she took as a hint to continue. "Come with me to the back room, and I will do everything within my ability to help you," she said, coaxing me to follow her. "I might be the only help you have. It would be such a shame for you to turn down the opportunity I'm giving you now."

I swallowed, trying to absorb what she was saying. "Do you mean you can help me get Drew back?" I asked.

"That might be something I can help you with." She leaned closer to me, her eyes taking on a sinister quality. "If you're willing to listen."

Shannon seemed as intrigued as her aunt to hear my decision, and from the determination in her eyes, I got the feeling I might risk losing her as a friend if I didn't listen to what Genevieve had to say. I would hate if that happened. Now that Lizzie had gone behind my back and destroyed any trust I had in her, Shannon was the closest thing to a friend I had. I always dated lots of boys, but never had any close friends who were girls besides Lizzie. I hadn't needed anyone else. Now if Shannon got mad at me, she might tell everyone in her group not to be friends with me. Then I would have no one.

The thought of being alone frightened me more than I cared to admit.

"Alright," I decided. "Let's do this."

CHAPTER 4

*Genevieve led me into the back room, which was the size of a large walk-in closet. It smelled old and musty, like it hadn't seen fresh air for years. A dark Persian rug was spread out on the floor, and there was a small wooden table with colored candles on it and a crystal ball in the center. Around the table were two worn red velvet chairs. The room was dim, the only light coming from the standing lamp on the side of the room with a pink cloth shade. Next to the lamp was a cabinet with a teakettle on top of it.

"Please take a seat, dear," Genevieve said, motioning to the chair farther from the door.

It was only the two of us now. This talk about what Genevieve referred to as "past life regression" was a private matter, so Shannon had to wait in the store while Genevieve did whatever witchy-voodoo thing she was going to try with me.

At the very least, this situation had entertainment value. Not like I would be able to joke about it with anyone. That would require admitting I was here in the first place, which was out of the question.

I followed Genevieve's instructions and sat in the chair, resting my elbows on the armrests. She leaned her cane against the wall and dimmed the lamp. Then she went into the cabinet, pulled out a blue ceramic mug, and poured some tea into it. After she finished, she picked up the steaming hot mug and maneuvered into her seat.

"So, how do we do this?" I asked, not bothering to hide my amusement. Just because I was going along with this wacko plan didn't mean I had to pretend to believe that what she said about past lives was possible.

She placed the mug in front of me, then struck a match, lighting the three candles on the table. The strong smell of incense filled the room. I looked down into the mug. The drink inside of it was colored like cinnamon tea, only it didn't smell like cinnamon. It smelled sweet, but a little bitter, too. I had no idea what it was. I didn't have anything against tea, but I'd always been more of a coffee girl.

"First you have to drink the tea and try to relax,"

Genevieve said, blowing out the match and placing it in the tray beneath the center candle. "I understand you're skeptical, and you don't believe what I have to tell you. However, I want you to open your mind to the possibilities. If you do, then you may receive the help you desire. Can you do that for me?"

I pressed my lips together, thinking about it. What if Genevieve *could* help me get back together with Drew? Wasn't it worth giving her a chance?

"I guess I can," I answered.

Genevieve looked content with my response. Then she motioned to the tea. "Drink," she said.

I picked up the mug, blowing in it before taking a sip. The tea was hot, and it didn't taste terrible. It wasn't good, either. It reminded me of berries, but how I imagined they would taste if they weren't quite ripe yet. Genevieve watched me as I drank, and I drank it quickly, since it was awkward sitting there drinking with her not talking to me. Once finished, I placed the empty mug back down on the table and waited for her next instructions. The tea was warm and soothing, and even though my head felt foggy, I couldn't remember ever feeling so relaxed in my life.

"Now I want you to close your eyes," Genevieve said. "Put every thought you have out of your mind, relax, and focus on what I'm saying."

I followed her instructions, closing my eyes and leaning back into the velvet chair. The candles had a raspberry smell, and I sank into the seat, easily falling into complete relaxation.

Before I knew what was happening, images from the past few months filled my mind. I remembered when Drew walked into class on the first day of school with his black leather jacket and dark mussed up hair. I remembered the fun times we had together—hanging out at my house after our first date at the movies, sitting on the back bleachers during the Beech Tree vs. Derryfield soccer game, and when he told me during lunch that I was the only person he wanted to eat with. He even played guitar for me when I was over his house. When I was with him, I felt wanted and special. I remembered how he said we could go to his house in Palm Beach over winter break, and skiing at his house in Aspen in the spring. With Drew, life was full of adventure and possibilities.

Now those things would never happen.

At that thought, the darker memories sunk in. How he used to zone out and refuse to tell me what he was thinking, how I caught him watching Lizzie during the soccer game, and the way he ran after Lizzie at Shannon's party, not thinking twice about me.

"Are you relaxed?" Genevieve's voice interrupted my thoughts.

I nodded, not moving as I waited for her to continue.

"Picture a white light surrounding you," she instructed. "See it in your mind first, and then around your arms, hands, body, legs, and feet, until it's enveloped you completely."

The image of a glowing white light instantly formed in my mind. It felt warm and tingly, and I could envision it spreading over my skin, making a protective cocoon around my body. It was like armor, as if it could stop anything bad from reaching me.

"Now I want you to picture a long hallway in front of you, with a large door at the end," she continued.

I didn't have to concentrate too hard before an image of a hallway formed in my mind. It looked like something from another time, with pale yellow walls and light wooden floors. Portraits of fancily dressed people who were too serious for their own good lined the walls, all within elaborate gold molded frames. They looked like they belonged in a museum. Most of the portraits were of individual people—women in high waisted gowns with their hair styled in curls atop their heads, and men wearing jackets and white shirts that went all the way up to their chins.

At the end of the hallway was a door, and it was more beautiful than any door I had ever seen. White marble columns flanked both sides, and an arch designed with intricate carvings formed over the top. On both sides of it were small wooden tables holding golden candelabras. It looked like it led somewhere majestic and magical.

"I want you to walk toward the door." Genevieve's voice sounded far away and dreamlike, like an echo through the hall. "When you get there, turn the knob and enter wherever it may lead."

I did as she said and took a few tentative steps toward the door. The white light around me grew more intense, as if it was trying to protect me from whatever I was about to walk into.

I reached for the golden knob, gave it a gentle turn, and slowly opened the door.

CHAPTER 5

On the other side of the door was a beautiful ballroom from another century. The floor was tiled with white marble, and the two-story walls were lined with Ionic columns. Huge windows filled the far wall, surrounded by heavy, gold-colored drapery tied back with large tassels. It was dark outside, and since there was no surrounding light I guessed the location of this place to be somewhere in the country. I looked up, amazed by the glass chandelier hanging from the ceiling —I'd never seen a chandelier so large in my life. But the strangest thing about it was that instead of being electric, it was lit by candles.

I didn't have time to think about it anymore, because people started to appear, blurry at first, and gradually coming into focus. They were dancing, and dressed from a different time. The women wore long, flowing dresses with empire waists, and the men wore fancy tuxedos and jackets. Most of the dresses were pastel, with puffy sleeves, and lots of the girls wore gloves that went up to their elbows. Many of them wore ribbons around their waists that tied in the back and went down the length of their dresses. A string orchestra played in the corner, and the classical music was so familiar—like I'd heard it before, but couldn't remember when. Even the dance felt familiar, with the women and men standing in lines across from each other, occasionally bringing their elbows together as they circled around each other. They were all talking, laughing, and having fun.

No one acknowledged me though. I supposed that even though I could see them, to them I was invisible.

The whole scene has a dream-like quality. I could hold onto it, but it felt like it could slip away without a second's notice.

I caught sight of a girl who looked like I might have if I'd lived back in that time. She didn't look exactly like me, but close enough that we could be sisters. Her hair was the same color as mine—dark brown with a hint of red—but piled into a mass of curls on the top of her head. She wore a beautiful red and gold gown, with an empire waist that flowed dramatically to the floor, and she had on white gloves that went all the way up to her elbows. She danced with a guy who resembled Drew, except his hair was longer. He was wearing a white shirt with a ruffled front that went up to his neck, underneath a fancy black jacket. They seemed to be the center of attention, smiling at each other like they couldn't be happier. The scene felt so familiar, like it was something I had once experienced myself.

Then a girl walked inside the ballroom who looked strikingly similar to Lizzie. She had the same golden curls, and her long white dress was plain compared to the others in the room. She wore no gloves or jewelry. Drew saw her as well, but before I could see more of the scene, it blurred and shifted, turning into something else.

Now the girl who resembled me and the guy who looked like Drew were walking through a garden, talking about something serious. The scene wasn't as clear as the one in the ballroom, and I had no idea what they were discussing. Something was pulling me back. It was like being underwater, where everything sounds fuzzy and when you open your eyes to see, the world has a surreal, blurry quality.

I wasn't supposed to be there, but I held on, wanting to know more.

The scene flashed to my and Drew's lookalikes inside an old house. He looked devastated, and I couldn't

MICHELLE MADOW

imagine what had happened to him. Then it switched again, and what I saw in front of me was unmistakable. It was a wedding. My and Drew's past selves stood at an altar in a magnificent church as they exchanged vows. The fuzziness made it hard to see their exact expressions, but it didn't matter. I knew what I was seeing, and it meant I was right.

Drew and I were supposed to end up together.

Then I was yanked back to the present, to the room in the back of Mystic Pathways. My eyes snapped open, and I gasped as though I had emerged from the water after trying to see how long I could stay under.

What had I seen? I watched the flames of the candles flicker in front of me as I reoriented myself, sorting the images as they played through my mind. I knew they couldn't be real, but they felt like it. It was like they were memories, but ones I hadn't experienced myself.

It could only mean … but no, that was impossible. Still, I couldn't shake the thought.

The memories were ones I had experienced in another lifetime.

"What did you see?" Genevieve asked. She watched me closely, her eyes glowing in anticipation as she waited for me to respond.

"It's impossible." I shook my head, unable to accept it. However, the images remained in my mind, as real as if

30

they had actually happened. I had no idea how to handle this. I wanted to forget what I'd seen, but I couldn't force the memories out of my head. There was no turning back.

"Rare, but not impossible," Genevieve said. "Reincarnated souls don't come around often. It's my job to help them recall their past lives, and help them in their current one. And you, my dear, are in much need of my help. So tell me..." She leaned forward, pressing the tips of her gnarled fingers together. "What did you see?"

Unable to keep it to myself, I told her about the scenes, giving as many details as I could. She listened intently, nodding here and there, pleased as I described everything. The strangest thing was, as much as I barely believed it, I couldn't deny what I'd seen.

I lived a past life, and in that life I married Drew. Even though every logical part of my brain told me it was impossible, it felt real. I told myself it was ridiculous, but that didn't matter. The feeling wasn't something I could make go away. And I wasn't sure I wanted it to.

"Very interesting," Genevieve said once I finished. "But in this life things don't seem to be working out the same way, do they?"

"No," I said, sitting back in disappointment. My chest tightened at the memory of Drew running after Lizzie at Shannon's party, and of Lizzie telling me she thought she and Drew were "meant to be." If only she knew what I had seen—that in the past Drew ended up with me, not her. I doubted she would act all high and mighty then. "Even when Drew and I were together, there were times he would act distant, and he wouldn't tell me what he was thinking. Then he started to pull away, and no matter how hard I tried, I couldn't get him back. It was all because of her—Lizzie." I sneered when I said her name. "It's like she put a spell on him. He's entranced by her, and I have no idea how to make things right between us."

"And what if I told you I could help?" Genevieve asked.

"I'm listening." I folded my hands on my lap, waiting for her to elaborate. I wasn't sure what she could do for me, but I was out of other options. I was willing to do anything at this point.

She got up and walked to a wicker basket in the back of the room, opening it and pulling something out. It was a vial, capped shut and filled with tinted red liquid. It looked like diluted cranberry juice. She held it to her forehead, closing her eyes and muttering something I couldn't understand, and then walked back over to the chair to sit again.

"Take this," she said, holding the vial out to me. "It's

something special I made myself, with the expectation that someone who needed it would be coming to me soon."

I reached to take the vial from her, surprised by its warmth. "What is it?" I asked. "And what do I do with it?" Capped shut with a rubber top, it was like something from a laboratory. I swished it around. The liquid inside was about the same consistency as water.

"Tonight is the full moon." Genevieve's eyes took on that chilling look again. "You want things in this life to end up the same way they did in your past life, don't you?"

"Yes." I nodded. "I do."

"Then what you have to do is simple," Genevieve said. "First you must drink the solution. It's very important you do that before the other steps. Then you will light a candle—I'll give you one. After the candle is lit, write your wish on a piece of paper. Word it *exactly* as I say." She paused for a second, watching me closely to let me know how serious she was about this part. "You will write, 'I wish everything in this life between me, Drew, and Lizzie will end up the same way it did in our past life.' Once it's written, close your eyes and recall the images you saw in your past life regression. Focus on the way things ended with you and Drew in the past, and how you want it to turn out the same way in the present. Once you've recalled everything you saw, look into the flame and burn the paper with your wish on it. When the paper is gone, you may blow out the candle."

I stared at her like she'd lost her mind. "It sounds like you're asking me to cast a spell," I said, waiting for her to deny it. It was one thing to think about hallways and doors and seeing something that could *possibly* be a past life. But to drink potions, light candles, and burn papers with wishes written on them? That was way beyond my comfort zone.

"That's exactly what I'm asking you to do," she said, her voice flat and serious. "You wanted help, and I'm giving you what you need. Making that solution was not simple." She paused to examine the vial I held in my hand. "It's rare that I give someone such a valuable gift. At the very least, take it home and think about it. You have until sunrise to make your decision. If you don't go through with it tonight, then you will have to wait until the next full moon, and the solution will no longer be at its full strength."

I looked at the potion again, wondering what was in it. I had a feeling I didn't want to know the answer.

"Fine," I gave in. "I'm not going to promise anything, but I'll think about it."

"Good," Genevieve said, relaxing in her chair.

I couldn't help but wonder why she wanted me to do

this so badly. What was in it for her? Not that it mattered. If it helped me, that was all I cared about.

"Don't tell anyone about what we did in here today," Genevieve continued. "Not Shannon, and especially not Lizzie or Drew. They will try to tell you lies to confuse you, to make you doubt yourself, but you need to trust what you saw. As long as you do what I told you, fate will make sure everything ends up the way it did in the past. That's what you want, isn't it dear?"

"Yes," I agreed, holding the vial tighter in my hand. "More than anything in the world."

CHAPTER 6

*S*hannon must have understood that what went on between me and Genevieve in the back room wasn't supposed to be shared, because she didn't ask any questions about it while we shopped for the rest of the day. Even though I loved the mall, it was hard to focus on shopping after everything that had just happened. I had to remind myself when Shannon was speaking to me, and to respond appropriately. We ended up buying a few things, mainly in the form of clothing, and after a few hours decided to head back to her house. Shannon told me Amber was going to meet up with us there, and the three of us were going to hang out. She thought some girl time would help get my mind off everything. Maybe she was right. At least it was better than sitting around my house with nothing to do, waiting for the full moon.

I clutched my purse during the drive, the vial with the potion and the candle tucked inside. The idea of using the potion seemed ridiculous, but I wasn't against trying it. The worst that could happen would be it not working. Still, before I did anything drastic I wanted to know if this was something I could fix on my own, without outside help.

The only way to do that was by talking to Drew.

Gathering up my courage, I took out my cell phone to text him.

Are you busy right now? I wrote, pressing send without giving myself time to second guess what I was doing.

I hated being so forward—I usually let guys do the chasing—but I had to talk to him before doing Genevieve's spell tonight. Also, when Drew and I dated, we spent tons of time together. We ate lunch together every day, and after school I would go over his house and we would do homework. I'd thought of him not only as a boyfriend, but a friend as well. He owed me a better explanation about what he did, and why he did it.

I prayed he wasn't with Lizzie right now, but Lizzie and I had been friends for long enough for me to know she had dinner with her mom on Sundays. I hoped she was doing that instead of hanging out with Drew.

My phone buzzed a few seconds later, and my heart raced at the prospect of what he wrote back to me.

I'm not busy. What's up?

I smiled at the response. He could have ignored me, but he didn't. That had to be a good sign.

Coming back from the mall with Shannon. We're gonna hang out at her house for a bit. I've been thinking a lot about what happened in the past few weeks, and since you live so close to her, I was wondering if I could stop by for a few minutes. Just to talk.

I pressed send without re-reading it. His response arrived in less than ten seconds.

I'm not sure that's a good idea ...

My heart dropped when I read the message. But on the bright side, it wasn't a no. Maybe I still had a chance with him.

Just a few minutes? Lizzie came to talk to me last night, wanting to be friends again, but I couldn't. I want to talk to you to try to understand what happened, so I can forgive her.

It was a lie, but I sent it anyway. It didn't matter how I got to be alone with Drew—just that I managed to do it. From there, he would realize how much he missed me and what a bad choice he made ditching me for Lizzie. If Genevieve was right and we were together in the past, it made sense for us to be together in the present.

He couldn't fight fate.

When the phone buzzed with his response, I was afraid to see what he'd said. I forced myself to look anyway.

Okay ... you can come by. But I have homework to do for tomorrow, so you can't stay long.

It wasn't much, but I smiled anyway. It was finally time for me to make things right again.

"Can you drop me off at Drew's?" I asked Shannon.

"Is that who you were texting so furiously?" she asked.

"Yep." I tossed my cell into my purse. "He said he'll talk to me, and I can go over now. That's okay, right? I'll come back to hang out with you and Amber after I talk with him. Everything's been so hectic the past few days, and I haven't had time alone with him since your party ..."

"It's okay," she said. "You should talk to him. He lives two houses from mine—but since the houses are far apart, I'll get out at mine and you can take my car to his so you don't have to walk in the cold. That way I'll be home when Amber gets here."

"Thanks," I told her. "And thanks for everything else today ... bringing me to Genevieve's and all."

"No problem." Shannon laughed. "As long as you don't mention it to anyone at school."

"I won't," I assured her.

"But as a friend, can I give you some advice?" she asked. I knew she was going to give it anyway, so I nodded for her to continue. "Before you go to Drew's, you've got to do something about your hair and makeup."

CHAPTER 7

fter re-applying my makeup and running Shannon's CHI straightener through my hair, I pulled in front of Drew's house, nervous about whatever was about to happen. Even though he was my boyfriend first, now he was Lizzie's. I was betraying her by being over there.

I wiped the thought from my mind. Lizzie was the one who stole Drew from *me*. I had every right to be there.

If life really ended happily ever after like Lizzie believed, I would get the guy in the end. But life wasn't a fairy tale, and I had no problem doing what was necessary to get what I wanted, even if it meant playing dirty.

I felt sad for a moment, thinking about the friendship Lizzie and I once had. In elementary school we built forts out of blankets and pillows and staked claim to them, talking forever and not allowing our parents inside. In middle school, when we had sleepovers, we would do each other's makeup and hair, then stay up watching reality television and made-for-TV movies. At nighttime in the summer we used to walk to the park near my house and watch the stars. Lizzie would tell me what the constellations meant, and we would make wishes. I never believed they would come true, but I wished anyway. In high school, I saw less of her because she was dating Jeremy, but we still stuck by each other. Whenever I needed someone to talk to and ask for advice, Lizzie would be there for me, even if it meant talking on our cell phones late into the night when we had to wake up early the next morning. She was my only true friend.

I had no idea what made her change into a selfish, boyfriend-stealing brat.

I put Shannon's car into park and picked up my cell phone from my purse. *I'm outside*, I texted Drew.

Come in, he wrote back.

My stomach fluttered. I didn't know why I was nervous to see him. We dated for two months, and during that time we were around each other a lot. But things were different now. Back then I thought he wanted to be with me. Now he would be thinking about Lizzie when we were together. The thought made me feel sick. What did Lizzie have that I didn't? Why did *she* always get the guy?

The nervousness turned to anger at the reminder of everything that had happened in the past few weeks. I had every right to be at Drew's right now.

The freezing wind assaulted me the moment I stepped out of the car, and I wrapped my arms around myself in an attempt to stay warm. Next year I would apply to colleges in California, Arizona, Texas, and Florida. Then I would be able to wear cute dresses all year long and not have to deal with terrible winters. Lizzie and I started talking about colleges in warm climates over the summer, and even though I no longer wanted to go to the same college as her, a warm place was still the plan.

When I reached the huge wooden front doors of Drew's house, I was so cold my lips must have been blue. I raised my hand to knock, but the door opened before I had a chance.

I looked up into Drew's brown, gold-flecked eyes and froze on the spot. He was still tan even though it was almost December, and his hair was styled in his typical "messed up but still super hot" look. He wore dark jeans and a black shirt, and even though he wasn't wearing anything different, something about him seemed changed. I couldn't figure out what it was, but then it came to me. He looked more relaxed than usual. He looked … happy.

Happier than he had ever looked when he was with me.

"Do you plan on coming in, or are you going to stand on my steps and freeze to death?" he asked. He didn't sound glad to see me, but he didn't sound annoyed either. I had no idea what was going through his mind.

"I'm coming in," I said, taking a step inside.

Even though I'd been there a bunch of times, the magnificence of his house never ceased to amaze me. Everything in it was antique, except for the electronics and the modern furniture in Drew's room. It felt like stepping back in time.

He shut the door behind me, and I knew this was it. I had to come up with something to say to make Drew want me back.

But why would he want me back when he seemed so happy without me?

The thought made my eyes water, and I swallowed, blinking the tears away.

"So … how have you been?" I asked.

This was not getting off to a good start.

"Great, actually." He stuck his hands in the back pockets of his jeans and glanced out the window. I could tell he was uncomfortable. "What's this you were telling me about wanting to 'forgive' Lizzie?"

I took a deep breath and tried my best to gain my composure. Acting unsure of myself was no way to make Drew see that I was the one he should be with.

"That's not why I really wanted to come over," I said, strutting through the entrance hall as if I lived there. The jeans I was wearing made my legs look amazing, and I wanted to show them off. "Can we sit somewhere? Your room, maybe?" I turned to face him and curved my lips upward, raising an eyebrow suggestively. Maybe my natural charm would be enough that I wouldn't even have to use the potion to get him back.

His eyes darkened at the realization of why I had really asked to come over. "I don't think that's a good idea . . ." he trailed.

"Come on." I pouted. "Won't you at least hear me out? We were together for two months, and then I turn around to find you dating the girl I've been best friends with since elementary school. You owe me more of an explanation."

The scenes I saw while in the back room at Mystic Pathways flashed through my mind—the ones of Drew and me at the dance and then later at an altar—reminding me I was right to be here. The idea of past lives still seemed strange, but I knew what I felt. Drew and I were meant to be together. Fixing things between us shouldn't be hard.

"We can go to the family room," he decided. His tone was firm—there was no changing his mind. I also knew not to push it, since the last thing I wanted was to drive him away from me.

"Sounds great." I smiled.

He led the way to the family room, and I followed a step behind him. Memories from earlier in the school year flooded my mind. I remembered the first time he showed me his house, when he seemed so happy watching me admire everything as he took me on the grand tour. I wished everything between us now was as lighthearted as it was then. What had happened to change it all?

The answer came to me quickly—Lizzie. Luckily Drew's back was toward me, so he didn't see me sneer when I thought about her.

In the family room, an armchair and a couch faced a flat-screen television attached to the wall. Under the TV was a marble fireplace. My heart sank when Drew sat in the armchair. Not having much of a choice, I perched on the end of the sofa closest to the chair, crossing my legs in his direction. I read in Cosmo that this was a subtle way to let a guy know you were interested, and employed the technique whenever possible.

"So ..." he started, leaning back in the chair and tapping his fingers against the armrest.

I took that as a clue to start. "Were you and Lizzie together before we broke up?" I asked.

"No." He looked straight at me when he said it, and I could tell he was being truthful. At least that was a relief.

"Okay." I paused, hoping he would say something to continue the conversation. When he didn't, I asked, "How long were you thinking about wanting to be with her when we were together?"

I cringed after asking. It sounded like we were playing twenty questions or something lame—made even lamer by how I was the one with all the questions, and he didn't care to ask me anything.

Because he didn't care about *me*.

I pushed the thought out of my mind. It hurt too much to think about. He dated me first—he chose me first—which meant he had to care about me.

"I don't know." He sighed and ran a hand through his hair. "It just happened. I'm sorry, Chelsea. I shouldn't have dated you knowing how I felt about Lizzie. It was wrong. If I could go back in time and change it, I would, but I can't. It's just how it is." He paused, deep in thought, and continued, "Sometimes it's impossible to control how you feel about someone. That's how it is with me and Lizzie."

His words hit me hard. "Does that mean you wanted to be with Lizzie from the beginning?" I asked. "For the whole time we were together?"

He nodded. "I'm sorry," he said. "It wasn't fair of me, I know. But like I said, I can't change it now. Someday you'll find the right person for you, but that person isn't going to be me."

I sat back in shock, unsure how to respond. The worst part was that he seemed to mean it. He felt bad about how everything had worked out—but feeling bad wasn't going to cut it.

We were supposed to be together. Why couldn't he see that?

"There's nothing I can say to change your mind, is there?" I asked sadly.

"No." He managed a small smile—as if he was glad I was giving up. Yeah, right. If only he knew what was coming next. "It's hard to explain, but there's something right about me and Lizzie being together. It's the way things are meant to be. I know it's difficult for you to hear, but after everything I put you through, you deserve the truth."

"The truth being you want to be with Lizzie and not me." The words sounded hollow to my ears. "But tell me one thing," I started, even though I had a dreadful feeling I wasn't going to like his response. "Do you love her?"

"I do," he said. "Very much."

I deflated at his answer. "Okay," I said. "Thanks for telling me, I guess."

I could have tried harder. I could have done something bold, like flinging myself at him to see if he would push me away or not, but I had more dignity than that.

I also had the vial full of Genevieve's potion.

And what I planned on doing with that potion was all I thought about when Drew walked me to the door and said goodnight.

CHAPTER 8

The entire time Shannon, Amber, and I were hanging out at Shannon's house, I couldn't stop myself from glancing at my purse, thinking about the vial inside. At least they didn't pry too much about what happened when I went to Drew's house. I think they could tell from the irritated vibe I was giving off that things didn't go well. Anyway, they were happy gossiping about the guys on the soccer team and Amber's crush on Jeremy. We had pizza delivered while we watched a movie (although we talked through most of the movie) and we made ice cream sundaes afterward. I normally didn't eat junk food, but I made an exception since the past few weeks had been awful.

I knew they were doing this to help me get my mind off the break-up, so I did my best to have a good time. But I couldn't forget about everything that had happened recently. By the time Amber offered to drive me home, I was more than ready to head out.

"This was fun," I said as Shannon walked us to the front door. "Thanks for dragging me out of the house today."

"Sitting home sulking is never good for anyone," Shannon said. "And going to the mall was helpful, right?"

"Yeah." I looked warily at Amber, not wanting her to know about Mystic Pathways. Even though the two of them were best friends, I had a feeling she didn't know about Shannon's connection to the store. "Very helpful. I'm glad we went."

"And how come I didn't get invited on this mall trip?" Amber crossed her arms and glared at Shannon.

"Would you have wanted to wake up before noon on a Sunday?" Shannon retorted. She raised an eyebrow, already knowing what Amber's response would be.

"Good point," Amber said. "I would have been pissed if you woke me up."

"Anything before 1:00 PM is early for Amber on the weekend," Shannon explained.

"I like my sleep, too," I said. "And honestly, you surprised me. I didn't peg you as a morning person."

"Sometimes people are full of surprises." Shannon laughed.

That was an understatement—Shannon was the last person I expected to be involved with mystic-psychic stuff.

And Lizzie was the last person I expected to go after my boyfriend behind my back.

It goes to show that no matter how close you think you are with someone, you can never know them completely.

"I'm so not in the mood for school tomorrow," Amber grumbled when we reached the door.

"I'm never in the mood for school," Shannon said.

"Is anyone ever?" I asked. They agreed.

However, school tomorrow morning felt a long way off. I reached into my bag and wrapped my hand around the warm vial, smiling at the feel of it.

To say the night was still young was the understatement of the century.

CHAPTER 9

My dad was getting ready for bed when I got home. After telling him about my trip to the mall and hanging out at Shannon's, I was able to go up to my room and get the privacy I'd need for what was coming next.

To make sure my dad was fast asleep when I started doing the spell, I killed some time watching two shows I'd recorded on my DVR. I wasn't focused on the shows though—my thoughts kept wandering to the conversation I had with Drew at his house. Not only did he look happy, but he said he was happy, too. The entire time we dated, I'd never seen him quite so relaxed and content as he was now. Did I really have a right to take that away from him, to control him with Genevieve's spell?

Then I reminded myself of what I'd seen of the past. Drew and I were meant to be together. I wasn't sure why things were different this time around—why he thought he loved Lizzie—but I knew this was all wrong. Even though Drew thought he was happy, I didn't see how it could be possible. Once I put things back to the way they should be, he would realize his mistake. He would know he was supposed to be with me. In the end, what I was about to do would help him.

I hoped that was true with all of my heart.

I was sleepy by the time the shows were over, but I wasn't letting myself go to bed yet. I had important things to do. It was time to push my doubts aside and make things right again. Drew would soon realize he's supposed to be with me, and Lizzie would finally know how it feels to have the guy you love choose your best friend over you.

The kind of love that transcends time doesn't come around very often. I wasn't about to lose it.

I picked up my purse, took out the vial filled with the red liquid and the candle, and put them on the floor in front of my full-length mirror. I placed a plate under the candle so the wax wouldn't drip on my carpet. Even though Genevieve didn't tell me to sit in front of a mirror while doing the spell, it felt right. Then I went over to my desk to get a small piece of paper from my notepad, a pen, and a matchbook I'd taken from a Chinese restaurant a few years ago.

The red mask I'd worn to the Halloween dance was on the floor where I'd left it that morning. It was a beautiful mask, a swirled pattern in a mix of red and gold, continuing up over my forehead in leaf-like shapes with sparkling white gems. I held it up to my face and looked in the mirror. I had turned the overhead light off in my room so only the lamps were on, and in the dim lighting with the mask covering the top half of my face, I looked like the type of person who would do a strange spell in the middle of the night on the full moon.

I looked powerful—in control of my destiny.

I put the mask back on my desk and sat cross-legged on the carpet, studying the items in front of me. Genevieve said the first thing I had to do was drink the potion. I lifted the vial and held it up until it was right in front of my face, studying it. This was the part I was most hesitant about. Who knew what she put in there? For all I knew, it was her blood.

I shivered at the thought.

Not wanting to work myself up over ridiculous ideas, I uncapped the vial and held it up to my nose. It didn't smell bad. It had no smell at all. For all I knew, it was water with red dye in it. I held it up to my lips and took a sip to prepare myself before drinking the whole thing. It had a tangy taste, and it made the tip of my tongue tingle. I swallowed, and it felt warm and soothing as it slid down my throat. The taste reminded me of Scotch—one of the guys I dated last year stole some from his dad's liquor cabinet and insisted I try some—but the difference was this wasn't quite as strong, and it didn't have the intense flavor of alcohol.

After the first sip, I finished the rest in one gulp. Suddenly my body was on fire. The heat coursed out of my chest and pumped through every vein in my nervous system. My cheeks flushed, and I felt like I had in fifth grade when I got the flu with a 105-degree fever. I closed my eyes and held my breath for a few seconds, unsure of what to do. Luckily the heat subsided in less than a minute, turning into an ebbing warmth that filled my body.

It would have been nice if Genevieve had warned me about that beforehand.

I put the cap back on the now-empty vial and placed it next to me. One step down, a bunch more to go.

It took me two tries to get the match to light. Once lit, the candle let off a calming, raspberry smell. Then, using the silver Tiffany pen my dad got me for my birthday last year, I wrote on the piece of paper, making sure it was exactly how Genevieve phrased it:

I wish that everything in this life between me, Drew, and Lizzie will end up the same way it did in our past life.

The words flowed out of me easily, and I stared at

the paper after I'd finished writing the sentence, making sure I got it right. I wanted more than anything for this to work. To set things straight again, and make them the way they were supposed to be. The way they would have been if Lizzie hadn't stolen my boyfriend and messed up my entire life.

I placed the pen down and picked up the paper, reading it again before closing my eyes. Now I was supposed to remember everything Genevieve helped me see earlier today.

The flashes returned to me easily. The first one of the elegant ballroom, of the way Drew looked at me, as though I was the only person in the world. Him holding me close while we danced that night, in the center of the crowd as if we owned the room, the string orchestra seeming to be playing just for us. The two of us walking through the garden as he confided in me about something important. Then I saw the memory of the two of us in the old church, our families and friends gathered in the pews as they watched us on the altar. This memory didn't feel as happy as the others—something was wrong—but I did my best to ignore it. All that mattered was Drew choosing me in the end.

I was going to get that ending again.

I opened my eyes and looked at myself in the mirror. The light from the candle glowed against my face, warm on my tanned skin, bringing out the red in my hair. I smiled at my reflection. The warmth from the potion still filled me, making me feel as though I could do anything, as though I could make anything happen if I wanted it enough.

I wanted it more than enough. I wanted it with every fiber of my being, and I had the power to make it happen—to make it so I was the one Drew wanted, not Lizzie.

I picked up the paper and held it near the flame. For emphasis, I stayed focused on my reflection, and said the words aloud:

"I wish that everything in this life between me, Drew, and Lizzie will end up the same way it did in our past life."

Then I held the paper over the flame and burned it until ashes remained. When I finished, I blew out the candle.

Thunder boomed outside, followed by a flash of lightning so bright it lit up my entire room.

I had no proof, but I knew it worked.

And I couldn't wait to go to school tomorrow.

~

Thank you for reading *Vengeance*!

Now, turn the page to see the cover, description, and sneak peak of the final part of The Transcend Time Saga, *Timeless*! Or you can order it now by CLICKING HERE.

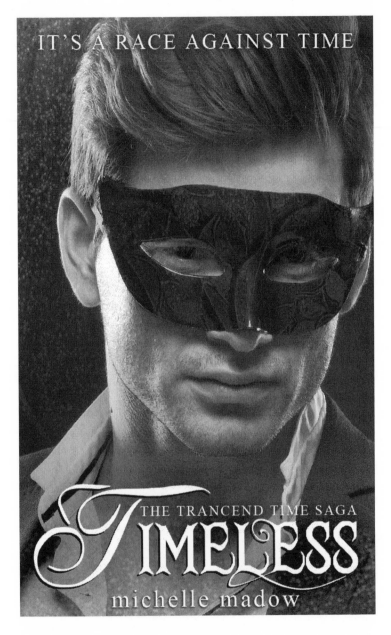

IT'S A RACE AGAINST TIME

THE TRANCEND TIME SAGA
TIMELESS
michelle madow

TIMELESS

THE TRANSCEND TIME SAGA: PART THREE

It's a race against time.

In Remembrance, Lizzie and Drew changed the course of fate so they could be together.

In Vengeance, Chelsea set fate back on its original, deadly path.

Now, strange things keep happening to Lizzie. Things that are omens of darkness to come. A curse has doomed her to die an early death, just as she did in her past life. To make matters worse, even if she can figure out who cast the curse, it's irreversible. There's only one option left for her to save herself. It's crazier than anything she's heard yet, and to do it, she'll need Drew and Chelsea's help.

Because to make things right, they must travel back in time to when it all began... and Lizzie discovers that the final events in her past life were more sinister than she ever imagined.

Turn the page for your sneak peak!

CHAPTER 1

"*I* can't believe you've never made s'more's before," Drew said, jabbing a marshmallow with an iron s'more stick and handing it to me.

"Not all of us went to fancy summer camps when we were younger where we made s'mores and sang Kumbaya around a campfire." I laughed and took the stick from him. Luckily we weren't sitting outside—New Hampshire at the end of November wasn't conducive to that, and I hated the freezing cold. Instead, we sat in front of the fireplace in Drew's living room, surrounded by a bag of marshmallows, a Hershey's chocolate bar, and a box of graham crackers. The living room was huge, probably as big as half of my house, and being in there felt like being back in time. The furniture was French antiques, and the hardwood floor was covered with a soft, woven Turkish rug. I loved curling up my toes and feeling the softness of it underneath them. With the fire blazing and Drew sitting next to me, I felt happier than I had in years.

"That wasn't all what my summer camp was about," Drew said as he prepared his marshmallow on the stick. "We also played sports, and did color war."

"What's color war?" I asked.

"My camp colors were blue and buff, and at the end of the summer we were assigned to one of the colors as a team. We would do cheers and play games against each other."

"I have a hard time picturing you cheering for a color team." I laughed.

"I got into it when I was younger," he said. "You should have seen it. I put zinc on my cheeks and everything."

"You'll have to show me a picture," I told him.

"I will later," he promised.

I looked into his dark brown eyes, the light of the fire reflecting against the flecks of gold inside them. After everything we'd been through in the past few months, it was hard to believe we were here now, making s'mores and talking about our lives. When I first saw Drew, he seemed so familiar to me, but I couldn't place where we'd met. I felt a connection to him, but I was dating Jeremy at the time, so I couldn't act on it. I also couldn't act on it because for the first two months after we met, Drew pretended like he wanted nothing to do with me. He dated my best friend, Chelsea, and avoided interaction with me as much as possible.

I didn't understand what I'd done to offend him so badly, and it hurt to be treated like that. But as much as I told myself that I shouldn't want anything to do with someone who acted that way toward me, I couldn't bring myself to dislike him. The undeniable connection I felt toward him wouldn't allow it.

Then I started having flashes of memories from a life long past—a life I'd lived in Hampshire, England in 1815. A life I'd shared with Drew.

Or a life I would have shared with Drew, if I hadn't suffered an untimely death in a carriage accident, destroying any chance we had to be together in our past lives.

Because I, Lizzie Davenport, an average high school junior at the Beech Tree School in Pembrooke, New Hampshire, have been reincarnated. It's still strange to think about. There are days when I wonder if it's actually possible, that I have memories of a life lived in a time so different from my own. Things like that are fun to read about in stories, but knowing it happened to me is beyond belief. But then I see Drew, and I know that the love we share is stronger than just this life—it runs all the way from the past into the present.

It turned out that our love wasn't the only thing that still existed from the past—the tragic end I'd suffered back then was trying to happen again as well. But after I narrowly avoided death in the present, when I stopped Jeremy from getting the two of us into an awful car accident that would have paralleled the carriage accident in the past, Drew came clean to me about why he'd been determined to avoid me. He thought if he didn't allow us to be together in current day, it would prevent the past from repeating, and stop my death from happening again.

But his avoiding me didn't work. Because seeing Drew for the first time made my memories of the past we shared bubble to the surface, and after a vivid flashback at the Halloween dance, I approached him about what I was seeing. He confirmed that yes, we were together in the past, although he hid his knowledge of my death. At first I was angry he withheld such important information, but now I understand why he did it—knowing that you died young and might die young again is a tough thing to process.

Since we stopped the accident from happening again,

we were now safe to be together, without having to worry about the possible death stuff. It was relaxing to be able to enjoy my time with Drew. The two of us could finally be normal teenagers.

Well, as normal as teenagers can be after realizing they were reincarnated to have another chance to be with their one true love.

I held the stick with my marshmallow over the fire. It hovered over the flames, the edges turning light brown. Drew took another approach, shoving his straight in. A few seconds later, he brought it out and blew out the fire surrounding his marshmallow. The outside was charred crisp. I had no idea how he could think that tasted good.

"What're you thinking about?" he asked, squishing his marshmallow between the graham crackers. Even though it was burned on the outside, it was gooey and soft on the inside.

"Just about everything that's happened," I said, rotating my marshmallow to evenly distribute the heat. "I still feel terrible about Chelsea. She had no idea about the history between us, and now she hates me ..." A lump formed in my throat, and I swallowed it away. Drew was my soul mate, but Chelsea was also my best friend.

At least she was until Drew and I told her we were

together. Now she refused to be in the same room as me. Thinking about how much I'd betrayed her made me feel sick. But I couldn't just not be with Drew, the person I'd been reborn to spend this life with. Anyway, Chelsea's reasons for wanting to be with Drew were superficial. All she seemed to care about were his looks, and her fascination with his growing up in New York City. It was like being known throughout school as "Drew's girlfriend" was more important to her than actually being with him and getting to know him.

What made me feel terrible was that I handled it wrong. I should have been honest with Chelsea about my feelings for Drew from the start.

But I couldn't change the past, so I had to focus on moving forward.

"She'll get over it," Drew assured me, draping his arm around my shoulders. "You just need to give her time."

"Speaking of time," I said, "We need to make sure I'm back home by 10:00. Curfew on school nights and all." I glanced at my watch, squinting at the face of the clock when I saw it said 5:15. But the sun had set hours ago. That couldn't be right.

"That's strange," I said, lifting my marshmallow away from the fire to tap the glass surface of the watch.

"What?" Drew asked after taking a huge bite of his s'more.

"My watch stopped."

"It probably needs a new battery," he said.

"But I got the battery replaced last month."

"Maybe you got a bad battery."

"Yeah." I shrugged, unable to come up with another reason. "That must be it."

Since my watch wasn't working, I checked the time on my phone. 9:20. Drew and I had thirty minutes together before I had to drive back so I got home before curfew.

"We'll get it fixed after school tomorrow," Drew said. "Okay?"

"Okay," I said, my thoughts returning to where they were before I noticed my watch had stopped. "I keep thinking about Chelsea, though. She's not the kind of person to forget about how we hurt her—even if neither of us did it on purpose. What if she never wants to be friends with me again?"

"If she doesn't want to be friends with you anymore, then she doesn't deserve your friendship," Drew said, finishing his s'more. "And besides, you have friends other than Chelsea. You were telling me the other day how you wanted to spend more time with Hannah, and you and Keelie are hanging out now, too. Both of them are nicer than Chelsea, anyway."

"You would know," I said. "You dated her."

"Hey." Drew nudged me with his shoulder. "I thought you were over that."

"I am," I said, pulling my marshmallow away from the flame. "And I know you never loved her. I just ..."

"Wish I had been honest about everything from the beginning," Drew finished my sentence. "I'll say 'I'm sorry' a million more times if that will make you forgive me."

"I've already forgiven you," I said honestly, looking into his brown eyes with the familiar flecks of gold around the pupils. "I love you too much to not forgive you."

"And I love you, too," Drew said, touching the silver heart bracelet he gave me yesterday. "Always and forever."

Drew helped me make my s'more, although unlike his, I didn't put a bar of chocolate in mine. I'm one of the few people—okay, the only person—I know who doesn't like chocolate, or sweet foods in general. Jeremy thought it made me a freak of nature. I was only tolerating the marshmallow because it was fun to cook in the fireplace.

Drew remembered how I didn't like chocolate in my past life, either, and he thinks it's cute. I'm not sure how not liking chocolate can be cute, but to him it is.

I didn't say anything as I ate my s'more, surprised

that I liked it. This was definitely something I missed by going to a church art camp instead of an outdoor sports camp like the one Drew attended. Once finished, I wiped my lips to make sure there wasn't any gooey marshmallow stuck onto them.

"I think my mom is dating someone," I said, stabbing a second marshmallow with the s'more stick.

"Is that a weird thing?" Drew ate his burned marshmallow right off the stick. Apparently we were done making them into marshmallow/graham cracker sandwiches, and were now eating them straight. It was less messy that way, and the good part was the marshmallow, anyway.

"Not weird," I said. "She dates sometimes. But it's never anything serious, and she always tells me about the guy she's going out with. I've gotten run-downs on all of her past dates. But she's being so secretive about whoever it is she's seeing now, and I can't help but wonder why."

"You should ask her," Drew said, like it was the simplest solution in the world. And when he said it like that, it did sound that way.

"Yeah." I rotated my s'more stick to cook the other side of the marshmallow. "I will."

Drew reached for the bag full of marshmallows to put another one on his stick. Then I heard a strange sound from the chimney—like something was trying to come through. A frantic flapping, followed by a loud squawk that sounded like a bird.

I didn't have time to ask Drew what was going on before a huge black crow slammed into the fire.

I yanked my s'more stick out of the flame and backed up on the carpet, with no idea what to do. The bird's feathers caught fire, combusting around its body. Its eyes were filled with panic. I wanted to reach in and save it, but I couldn't put my hand in the flames. Plus, the bird had already stopped moving. I had a feeling it was past the point where it could be saved.

Then I noticed a sickening smell—burning flesh. I covered my nose with my hand, not wanting to breathe in the aroma of death. I felt like I was going to be sick. I wanted to look away, so I didn't have to see the painful last moments of the poor animal being burned alive, but I couldn't pull away from the grisly scene. All I could see was the crow's hollow eye socket staring at me. Blaming me. Like it was saying, "You're next."

I shook the thought away—it made no sense. Why had I thought something so gruesome?

"Go into the kitchen." Drew's voice entered my panicked thoughts. "I'll take care of this." He grabbed my shoulders and forced me to look away from the dead bird in the fire. But not seeing it didn't erase the smell. Cooked flesh. Burning feathers.

The overwhelming aroma of death trapping me, leaving me no room to escape.

∼

CLICK HERE to buy *Timeless* and continue reading now!

ABOUT THE AUTHOR

Michelle Madow is a USA Today bestselling author of fast paced fantasy novels that will leave you turning the pages wanting more! Click here to view a full list of Michelle's novels.

She grew up in Maryland and now lives in Florida. Some of her favorite things are: reading, traveling, pizza, time travel, Broadway musicals, and spending time with friends and family. Someday, she hopes to travel the world for a year on a cruise ship.

To get free books, exclusive content, and instant updates from Michelle, visit www.michellemadow.com/subscribe and subscribe to her newsletter!

michelle@madow.com

45479059R00050

Made in the USA
Middletown, DE
16 May 2019